NIGHT RABBITS

To Daddy, with love and thanks for the summers at Huckleberry Hill
—*L.P.*

For Morgan, "The Bug"
—*M.M.*

Published by
PEACHTREE PUBLISHING COMPANY, INC.
1700 Chattahoochee Avenue
Atlanta, Georgia 30318

PeachtreeBooks.com

Text © 1999 by Lee Posey
Jacket and interior illustrations © 1999 by Michael G. Montgomery

First trade paperback edition published 2007

Book and cover design by Michael G. Montgomery and Loraine M. Joyner

Printed in June 2023 by Toppan Leefung in China

10 9 8 7 6 5 4 3 (hardcover)
10 9 8 7 6 5 4 3 2 (trade paperback)

Library of Congress Cataloging-in-Publication Data
Posey, Lee.
Night rabbits / Lee Posey ; illustrated by Michael Montgomery. —1st ed.
p. cm.
Summary: When her father becomes annoyed with the rabbits that are eating his carefully tended lawn at their summer cabin, Elizabeth tries to decide how to help because she loves the rabbits.
ISBN 1-56145-164-9
[1. Rabbits—Fiction.] I. Montgomery, Michael, 1952–   ill. II. Title.
PZ7.P838175Ni 1999
    [E]—dc21   98-34021
                                                                          CIP
                                                                          AC

NIGHT RABBITS
Written by LEE POSEY

Illustrated by

MICHAEL G. MONTGOMERY

PEACHTREE

ATLANTA

"Oh no, Elizabeth. The rabbits are eating my new lawn," my father says one morning at breakfast, looking out the cabin window.

He has worked on that lawn all summer. He planted it in the spring and came to the cabin every week to water it. The grass has grown so thick it feels soft between my toes.

But my father still works hard on the lawn. He pushes the old lawnmower. Drops of sweat fly off his body like water from the sprinkler. He rakes up the pine needles and bends over to pick up the pinecones.

When my father says the rabbits are eating his lawn, I am very quiet. I make sure that my spoon does not scrape the side of the bowl as I finish my cereal.

I love the rabbits.

Some nights at the cabin, I can't sleep. The crickets hum *zzzz mmm, zzzz mmm,* and the frogs answer back *ruumph, ruumph.* The noise keeps me awake, sticking in my mind the way the warm sheets stick to my body.

That is when I am glad the rabbits are here.

When it's so hot that I can't sleep, I get out of bed and go out on the porch. I swing quietly in the hammock and watch the rabbits.

They leap onto the lawn, then back into the trees, a dance of lighter shadows.

Their leaps are soft as shyness.

I think maybe there
are four rabbits, but I am
not sure. They are quick as
moonbeams.

I watch them jump up
high in the air with a flash
of their white tails, moving
to the music of the crickets
and the frogs.

The rabbits are so
beautiful that I shiver inside.

I watch until I can see them with my eyes closed. That's how I fall asleep.

I wake up back in bed, closer to morning, when everything becomes soft and gray, a picture waiting for the colors to be painted in.

My father's strong arms have carried me inside.

The night doesn't seem long and hot, not when I share it with my rabbits.

But now the rabbits are eating my father's lawn, and bare brown spots will grow like frowns.

I have an idea. That night after dinner, I get some lettuce. I leave it on the lawn, next to the pine trees where the rabbits hide, waiting for dark.

Now the rabbits can eat the lettuce, I hope, and not my father's grass.

When I walk back to the cabin, my father is standing in the doorway.

He puts his hand on my shoulder. "Is the lettuce for the rabbits?" I nod my head.

"They may not eat the lettuce. They may still eat the grass," he says. "That's just the way rabbits are."

I look up at him. He is smiling. His eyes sparkle like the lake when the setting sun turns the water gold.

"Some of those rabbits might have been born last spring, when I planted the lawn," he says. "They would be as old as the lawn is now. Maybe we can share the lawn with them, Elizabeth."

The next morning I know exactly what to do. After breakfast I go get a paper bag.

"What are you doing?" my father asks.

"I'll help you take care of the lawn," I say. "I'll pick up all the pinecones, and I'll pull all the weeds, too."

We pick up pinecones together.

Now when the sun has slipped behind the pine trees, the rabbits will dance on the lawn that belongs to them, to my father, and to me.